Mini Mia
and
Her Darling Uncle

For Lotta

Mini Mia

and
Her Darling Uncle

PIJA LINDENBAUM

Translated by
Elisabeth Kallick Dyssegaard

R&S
BOOKS

Stockholm New York London Adelaide Toronto

My mom and dad are in Miami.

Miami, where's that? I wonder. I didn't have to go.

I'm staying with Grandma.

My uncles are staying with her, too—all except Uncle Tommy.

He is almost always traveling.

I'm pretty sure my other uncles work in offices. Tommy doesn't.

My other uncles eat meat loaf all the time.

"That's just the way we like it," they say.

I like meat loaf fine.

But Tommy

prefers sushi.

Just then, the doorbell rings.

"Tommy!" I yell. "Is that you?"

"Darlings," says Tommy, just as sweet as always.

I'll get a present for sure. I always do when
Tommy has been away.

It's a dead snake in a glass jar.

"Oh, no," says Grandma.

But I've always wanted one.

I get to spend the entire time with Tommy.
I can forget about daycare.
"Mini Mia," says Tommy. "I have to
have time to relax, too."
He calls me Mini Mia. That's because my
favorite soccer player is Mia Hamm.
My real name is Ella.

Tommy loves to spend time with me.
And he dyes my hair a different color every day, if I want.
We don't play a lot of soccer, because Tommy
isn't very good at it.
Instead, we go out and listen to music,
and one day we go to the opera.

Another day, we just stay home and play dead.
And once in a while, we go people-watching.
Or we jump on both feet everywhere we go.

But one day, someone is sitting in Tommy's kitchen
when I go over.
"Hi," he says. "Are you Mini Mia? I'm Fergus."
Fergus, what kind of a name is that? I think.
He looks boring. And his pants are ugly.
"Let's go," I say to Tommy.
"I just have to cut Fergus's hair first," he says.
"Do you want me to color your hair today?"
No, I do not!

Fergus looks just as boring
with his new haircut.
And when we leave,
he tags along.
"Don't you have to go home?" I ask.
Apparently he doesn't.

We are going people-watching. But this is Tommy's and my hangout.
Now Fergus is standing there blabbering.
I don't understand what he is saying. He's from Scotland.
I think he should have stayed there.
"Want me to lift you up?" asks Tommy.
No, I am doing just fine down here, I think.
I pour sugar on Fergus's shoes.

Later, we go to the movies.

"I can't decide which movie I want to see," says Fergus.

But he doesn't need to know. Tommy and I only see sad movies.

I want sour cream and onion potato chips. We always share a big bag.

Fergus wants cheese crackers.

"Yes," says Tommy. "Good idea."

But, actually, I don't think I'll have anything.

Fergus obviously doesn't go to the movies much.

He doesn't get it.

Tommy is the only one who cries when a dog dies.

When the movie is over, we all need to pee and rush to the bathroom.
I get there first.
Then, it's Fergus's turn.
By then, I've gotten the whole roll of toilet paper wet.
Take that.

"should we go swimming tomorrow?" asks Tommy.
"Jerks," I say.
I'm not going swimming.
"Go home to Scotland!" I yell, and slam the door.

Now no one is allowed to talk to me,
and I don't want any dinner—just a little bit of jam.
I'm never going to hang out with Tommy again.
I'm just going to lie here. Bored stiff.
Forever.

But on Saturday, Tommy is standing there with his swim stuff.
And I can't help being pleased. Grandma is going shopping.
And I don't see Fergus anywhere.
Perhaps he died or stepped on a nail.

Just then, I see someone waving.
What a bad hiding place.
"Fergus is coming, too," says Tommy.
I'll pretend he doesn't exist, I think.

I get my own locker key because I'm old enough
to go into the women's locker room by myself.
Tommy and I jump into the shallow end.
Fergus heads straight for the deep end.
That's when I pull his towel into the water.
He doesn't notice, because he is heading
for the high diving board.

It's sooo high. Later, He stands up there
and clowns around.
He's obviously afraid to jump.
He bounces, but then leaps off.
Wow, cool, I think.
"How many points do I get?" asks Fergus
when he pops up.
"That was definitely a ten!" says Tommy.
Zero million, I think. But I don't say anything,
because I'm pretending he doesn't exist.

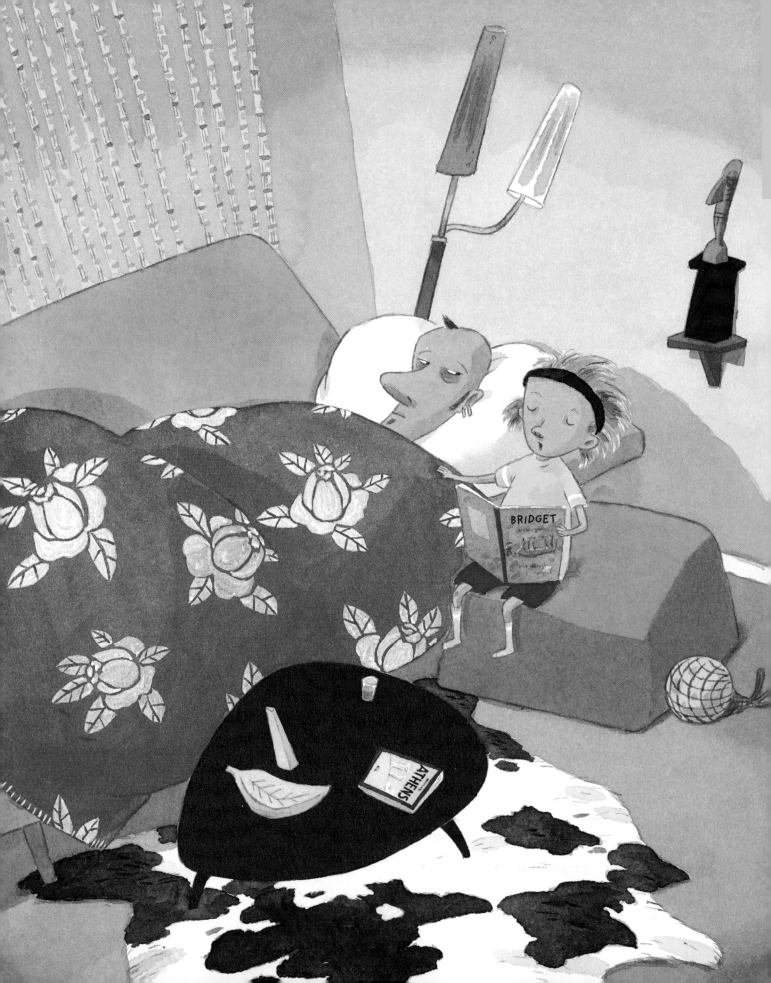

Later, Tommy starts to feel funny, so we have to go back
to his place.
He lies down on the couch and looks totally sick.
I pat his blanket a bit and give him some juice.
"Mini Mia," he says as he closes his eyes, "you'll have to hang
out with Fergus today."
I don't think so.
But I go out into the kitchen anyway.

Fergus has made cinnamon rolls. They are really burned.
As I knew they would be.
"Do you live here now or what?" I ask.
"No, not exactly," says Fergus.
After that, we can't think of anything else to say,
so we check out the paper.

Finally, Fergus says,
"Are you good at playing soccer?"
"Pretty good," I say.
"If you like, I can show you some shots."
I doubt it.
"Do you mind if I borrow that ball?"
I kick it a little.
"See you," he says, and then he just
takes off.

Now I don't even have a ball.
Do I have to sit here all alone as well?
Tommy is snoring.
From the yard, I hear the sound
of a ball bouncing.
Then I go out, too.

Fergus and I practice our shots all day.
When Tommy feels better, we play a game.
Tommy gets to be goalie since he is mostly in the way.
Fergus almost becomes the world champion.
But in the end I win!

Rabén & Sjögren Bokförlag, Stockholm
www.raben.se

Translation copyright © 2007 by Rabén & Sjögren Bokförlag
All rights reserved
Originally published in Sweden by Rabén & Sjögren under the title Lill-Zlatan och morbror raring
Pictures and text copyright © 2006 by Pija Lindenbaum
Library of congress control Number: 2006937074
Printed in Italy
First American edition, 2007
ISBN-13: 978-91-29-66734-9
ISBN-10: 91-29-66734-8

Rabén & Sjögren Bokförlag is part of
P. A. Norstedt & Söner Publishing Group, established in 1823